GW01018075

Printed in Scotland

First Printing, 2019
Second Printing, 2022

ISBN 978-0-9575917-4-5

Published by:
Maryhill Integration Network
35 Avenuepark Street,
Glasgow, G20 8TS

www.maryhillintegration.org.uk

Printed by:
The Print Box Scotland Ltd
1176 Argyle Street
Glasgow
G3 8TE
http://www.theprintbox.net/

Acknowledgements

We would like to thank everyone who has contributed their stories, experiences and views to this project, especially all the children from:

Knightswood Secondary School
St Fillan's Primary School
Evergreen Outdoor Nursery
Dunard After School Care

*Text in italics within the story are direct quotes from the children

Project Collaborators:
Pinar Aksu - Writer and Workshop Facilitator
Garry Mac - Illustrator
Tilly Gifford - Workshop Facilitator

Bouchra Boudelaa - Volunteer Workshop Facilitator
Saffanna Aljbawi - Volunteer Workshop Facilitator

Remzije Zeka Sherifi - Co-Producer, Maryhill Integration Network
Rachel McJury - Co-Producer, conFAB

A special note of thanks to the following people without whose support this book would not have been possible: Monica Cohen, Rose Filippi, Yağmur Aksu, Dee Heddon, and C Blaize.

The Swallows lived in a forest. A beautiful peaceful place. They were very happy in their home, surrounded by friends and family. Each morning when the sun rose, everyone would come together. They loved exploring the forest, finding new places and meeting new birds.

One day, the Swallow family awoke to the smell of fire and the fear of disruption. Deforestation had destroyed their home; everything was gone. The Swallow family were forced to leave their nests to search for a safer place.

They were left feeling completely hopeless. They did not know where they should go, how long the journey would take, how dangerous it might be or even if they would all make it. Unfortunately, they had no choice but to leave, they needed a new place to live.

After flying for what seemed an eternity, the Swallow family spotted a river and went to drink and search for food. They were exhausted.

The riverbank was eerily quiet and the Swallow family found it strange that there was no other wildlife around. The riverbank was a wasteland. A place of natural beauty had become polluted with oil and full of plastic debris. There was nothing to quench their thirst or give them energy for the next stage in their journey. Devastated, the Swallow family flew away.

COLA

Exhausted after several days of travel without food, they found a place to land. As they approached, they suddenly heard war planes piercing the sky and massive explosions, as bombs started dropping around them. Once a thriving place, it was now nothing more than a blanket of rubble.The Swallow family quickly flew away. Sadly, they were one less now.

The Swallow family spotted some mountains in the distance. They decided to stop.

Almost immediately, the Swallow family were filled with a disconcerting feeling. It was abnormally quiet and no birds were singing. As they looked around, they saw birds locked in cages.

The Swallow family discovered that those who had tried to speak freely were locked in cages. They heard stories of missing birds and saw military checkpoints. The Swallow family felt very unsafe and left the mountain.

Tired from the journey but still hoping to find somewhere safe they continued, heartbroken for the loved one they had lost. All those memories would stay with them forever.

Soaring through the wind and rain, they were joined by other birds. They asked themselves "Why are they leaving?" The Swallow family wondered what stories they had to tell.

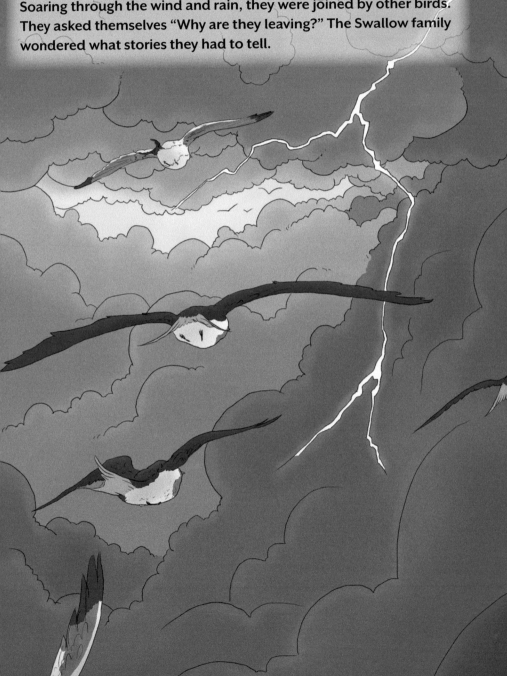

Going somewhere new is never easy. Speaking a different language makes communication very hard. Sometimes you feel you don't belong and you can't express your feelings.

Learning how everything works is interesting and challenging too. Visiting other nests, sharing and trying new foods can be very strange. Then you start missing your nest, where you had tall and shiny plants.

The Swallow family passed by many mountains and forests in search of safety and a new place to call home. They tried to survive in every possible way, eating anything they could find. In the evenings, they would find a safe branch to spend the night. They met new birds and interesting animals that they had never seen in their lives. Many other migrating birds would join them and share their stories.

Not everyone heals from homesickness. Sometimes you miss other places very much, you miss the people you have left behind. Homesickness is very painful.

The tree was alive with squawking and tweeting. At that moment, a Chiffchaff landed with its wagging tail, bringing silence amongst the tree.

When I was younger, the war started in my country and everything started to change. When our relatives began to leave and go to other countries, we became lonely and unstable. One day we were forced to leave too. It was difficult at first, because it is completely different in language, law and weather. As time went by, my father made every effort to work, but became sick and fatigued as it was very hard.

He decided to travel. The journey was very difficult and needed time, effort, and money. In the beginning we were unwilling to let him go. We were all tired and didn't want to remain alone in a strange country, where no one speaks our language fluently and we are unsure how the basic living expenses will get paid. But after while we agreed for my father to travel.

We were very sad to part, as we did not know when we would see him again. We prepared him for his mission with a little food and clothing in a backpack. He shouldn't carry much - perhaps he would spend a long time walking. My father had left. After two days he stopped talking to us and we were very worried. After a while we managed to contact him through one of the other travelers. He told us that my dad was fine but was exhausted by the tiring journey.

After a long period, we came to join him: we were reunited.

One parakeet, with smart beady eyes chirped and twittered from the top of the tree. The birds turned their attention to it.

One day, I went out with my four friends to have some fun together. The fun would not last.

At 7.30pm I returned home as I was late, leaving my friends behind. At 8.00pm I was resting. Suddenly I heard a very loud noise, there was terrible fire and screaming. My mum cried "Don't go outside!!". The lines were blocked, my friends weren't around. and I needed to find them. I ran out, to see what's happening. Lots of people were crying, shouting, running. I was shocked: it was like a piece of ice. Blood were lying on the floor. At that time, all I cared about was finding my friends. After a week they found their remains. This was last time I saw my friends.

A bird with colourful feathers and friendly eyes asked if anyone ever suffered from homesickness. Everyone raised their wings.

My best friend and I were fighting. But she went too far. She told me "why don't you go back to your own country?". After that it was never the same. I stopped eating and talking. I sat on my bed in my room for weeks. I was homesick.

I remembered it clearly: my gran standing, still waving like it was the last time I was going to see her. It was - she had a heart attack and passed away. I never healed from what happened. I talked to no-one, I lost all my friends. I was utterly alone. I hated the school, I hated where i lived. I hated that I left.

The moon was big
and bright that night.
Shadows could be
seen of other birds on
the branches. Many
stories were shared of
birds leaving home,
they spoke of loss and
loneliness, like the
Swallow family

Amongst all the stories
that evening, a place called
'Knotted Island' kept coming
up in conversation. A Goldfinch
mentioned that their cousin had
been living there for some time
now. Could this be the place to start
a new life and build a nest?

The very next morning, the Swallow
family set off with others in search
of Knotted Island.

The journey started with a thunderstorm, the birds lost sight of each other and many fell behind. No one knows what happened to them. As the Swallow family continued to fly, Knotted Island became visible in the distance.

Fighting through strong winds, the Swallow family were now within reach of the island. They had heard many stories about Knotted Island, how they would not be caged, but be listened to and have insects and worms to eat.

Getting closer, the Swallow family could not believe what they were seeing. The island had a huge immigration control net covering it, and walls separating the rivers and mountains. They wondered why so many barriers surrounded the much-talked about island?

Uneasy about what they could see of the island, the Swallow family decided to land on a rock nearby. From there, they saw two ducks being thrown out into the sea. Not sure why this was happening, they agreed to wait before going anywhere else.

They were very weak and tired from the journey and the pain they had witnessed. Not sure if they could continue flying any longer, they planned to stay on the rock and send one member of the family to the island.

From a distance, they spotted a small hole in the net which covered the island. The Wee One of the family volunteered and was small enough to fit through it, and so they would be the one to go and see what life on the island was like. They all promised to meet again at sunset to make a decision.

The Wee One, alone now, went through the net. Looking down on the island, the walls which separated the rivers and mountains became more visible. The island had so much greenery, tall trees and big lakes, but why are there so many walls on Knotted Island?

Keen to meet other migrating birds, it landed on a busy lake. The Wee One wanted to understand what it would be like to live here.

The Swallow family had suffered on their journey, they wanted to make sure the island would treat them well, allow them to build a nest, have food and share their beautiful songs with others.

The Wee One was amazed by the beauty of the lake which was very busy with many different and colourful birds. Some of the birds looked at the Wee One as it continued to wander around; worried about being seen, it decided to rest next to some reeds.

From a distance, an elegant Goose glided across the lake and approached the Wee One. "Welcome little one. Did you just arrive?"

Not sure what to say, the Wee One decided to trust the Goose and started to ask questions.

"Yes, yes, I just arrived. Earlier I saw two ducks thrown out of the island. I have my family waiting for me outside and need some advice. Please can you tell me what it was like arriving here, how did you feel, what is the process to settle and build a nest?"

The Goose could see its own reflection in the eye of the Wee One and was reminded of the time when it first came to the island.

"I arrived here many years ago now. I couldn't understand the other birds at first, they were singing a different language. I felt alone, in a bubble covered with darkness, others called me the loner. However, after a while, we started to understand each other - it was not easy at first, though with support and time we understood one another".

The Wee One was very curious to find out why this beautiful island was covered by a huge net which made it very difficult to enter.

The Goose started explaining the rules of Knotted Island. "Have you heard of the BigBirds? They control movement here. They built the walls and made the net to control the borders.

The BigBirds make migration and life very difficult for everyone. After all that we have suffered, after all that we have been through, the BigBirds want everything put down on paper. Other birds call the island 'The Land of Paperwork'."

The Wee One could not believe this. Why would the BigBirds build a net to control the island when there was plenty of space for everyone?

"The minute you land here, you need to inform the BigBirds. If you don't, then you could be in serious trouble.

When I first arrived, I had to go every week to the central control of the BigBirds called the 'Home Office' to 'sign-in'. The BigBirds make these appointments to monitor everyone. They search you and take your belongings, then you pass through a metal detector. If it makes a sound, the BigBirds get very angry. It may sound strange but it's all part of the hostile environment they create to make life very stressful and upsetting for those new to Knotted Island."

"I remember the Home Office very well" said the Goose, "there were large intimidating posters saying 'Is life difficult here? We can help you Go Back'. It was devastating to see these images around the room, we were already stressed and vulnerable. We left our homes to stay alive, but the fear of being sent back was killing us slowly.

Once, a family of ducks were late for their appointment, the ducklings were terrified when the BigBirds started shouting. I will never forget that moment, and the fear in their eyes.

When I used to go to sign-in, I was very anxious and worried; this is exactly what the BigBirds want, and they are rewarded for this.

This is only one story about the BigBirds, they use fear to control you. I suggest you speak with other birds to understand more about Knotted Island. If you wait here, I will send a friend over." The Goose stretched its wings out wide; it had some scars on each side, the Wee One didn't want to ask about them.

Up above, the sky began to turn grey, large clouds hid the sun and the first drops of rain began to fall on the big shiny leaves of the nearby plants.

A shy Robin approached, "You must be the Wee One, my friend asked me to visit you. Let me tell you this first, it's not going to be easy. The BigBirds make life very difficult for all new birds arriving here. For a very long time I hardly slept whenever we received the brown envelopes through the door, because we knew they were from the Home Office, bringing bad news. But one day, we finally received the news we were hoping for, that we could stay. I have to go now, but I wish you and your family good luck." The Robin disappeared.

Thinking about the BigBirds, the Wee One wandered around to ask more questions and learn more about the island.

From far away, the Wee One spotted a group of Flycatchers. They looked very busy, picking up berries and putting them in a safe place. The Wee One wanted to work as well. One of the Flycatchers, looking weary, was resting in the shade.

"It's amazing, everyone is picking up berries and working so hard", the Wee One said, "can I join you as well so I can get some insects and worms for my family?" Jumping up and down, the Wee One, was eager to hear what the Flycatchers had to say.

"What do you mean?" said one Flycatcher, "we are not allowed to work, only to volunteer. This means we work for free, and in return we can take a paper to the BigBirds to prove what we are doing. Everything here is about paper. But I'm tired. Not being able to work makes me feel worthless when I could so easily be able to support myself".

"To add to this injustice, the BigBirds don't even call us by our names, they call us Asylum Seekers. Look under my wing, it says Asylum Seeker. Until this is taken away by the BigBirds no-one will let me catch my own insects or worms, build a nest or offer my skills and knowledge; I have so much experience to share with others."

The Flycatcher left to help the others pick more berries. The Wee One felt upset and confused and didn't understand why so many birds were not allowed to catch their own food, or why the BigBirds made everything all about paper.

The sun came out from behind the clouds and it was bright once again. The Wee One noticed the constant change of weather on Knotted Island and how strange it was. Gathering some energy, it began to wander about again.

The Wee One spotted many Pigeons huddling together, shivering and asking for insects and worms from other birds.

The Wee One listened as one Pigeon told the others, "the BigBirds said I had to leave Knotted Island, but where can I go? I have been here for so many years now, my little ones were hatched here, they don't know about other places, this is their home.

Maybe one day the BigBirds will see that we belong here and allow us to build a nest and plan for our future; it would make Knotted Island a better place for everyone".

The Wee One left without saying anything. A friendly Magpie, with shiny green and blue feathers, landed on a branch nearby.

"Hello, you must be the Wee One, the Goose asked me to find you so you could meet others on Knotted Island at our Community Nest. You look tired, come with me, we have worms and water". The Wee One agreed to visit the Community Nest, but only for a short time.

The Wee One was welcomed by many birds. Feeling hungry, the Wee One had some worms and water. Wanting to find out more about Knotted Island before leaving, it wandered around the Community Nest.

"I'm lucky", said a Sparrow, "the BigBirds don't ask me questions as my grandparents have been here for many years now. I can catch my own insects, build a nest, travel and work freely. Although I'm still asked all the time, 'Where are you from?', when I say, 'From here, Knotted Island', they look at me and continue to ask 'But, where are you really from?' After a while you just learn to ignore it."

From the side of the nest, a Puffin waddled forward, looking down.

"I was in a cage for two months. The BigBirds checked on me every day. It was difficult, I could not move around or leave. It was very hard for me, being alone, not knowing when I would be free. The food was horrible and I was often moved to different cages. I was treated like a criminal, but I had done nothing wrong. I am free now, but I still cannot forget that horrible experience. I hope it will never happen to you. Here's a colourful good luck feather for you, I made this when I was in the cage."

The Wee One couldn't stop thinking about the giant cage that was full of so many frightened birds, and how it still exists to this day.

An excited Starling landed to explain what happened to its classmate, a Robin, "we heard our friend was at risk of being removed from Knotted Island, there were big blue vans with darkened windows. Our friend was very scared, their parents couldn't sleep and were very stressed. The BigBirds told them they would be sent to the cages, but they were not sure if this would be for a short time or indefinitely."

Today at school we collected lots of papers to support our friend Robin, saying it was unfair that our friend could be put in a cage and taken off the island"

The Wee One could feel the support in the Community Nest, looking around, it witnessed the strength of solidarity from all the different birds.

The Wee One thought about all the stories it heard at the Community Nest. It was not easy for anyone, the BigBirds made everything very difficult on the island. So many beautiful mountains and rivers divided by walls and covered with a big net. Thinking about all the friends it had made, the Wee One left to meet its family.

The Wee One slipped through the net and soared through the sky as the sun was beginning to set. Looking down it remembered those who can't work to catch their own food, or move freely, or build a nest.

With a heavy heart, the Wee One flew to meet its family. Everyone was anxious to hear all about what the Wee One had learned. Carrying the only worm it was given, the Wee One reached the rock they were waiting on, and noticed the tide was beginning to rise.

The Wee One tells them who it met, what the island looked like and who it was controlled by. They must decide soon what to do next as the family were very weak and it wasn't safe for them to stay on the rock.

It was too difficult for the family to try to make another journey and go somewhere else. The Wee One remembers all the solidarity, resilience and courage of the other birds, and so they decided to make their journey towards Knotted Island.

As the Swallow family reach Knotted Island, they are met by the screeching BigBirds with papers flying behind them.

The Wee One thinks, *we still have that smile of hope and a wish for a better tomorrow.*

THE END

Definitions

Asylum seekers
If you have claimed asylum in the UK, but have not yet had a decision on your case, you are an asylum-seeker. In legal terms, you are only a 'refugee' once your asylum claim has received a positive decision.

Detention
The Home Office changed the name of detention centres – where people subject to immigration control can be held – to 'immigration removal centres'.

Destitution
Destitute migrants are those without an income (not allowed to work or no access to financial support) and are often homeless. Access to services like medical care and education can be very difficult if you are destitute.

Deportation
Globally, 'deportation' refers to any enforced immigration removal.

Indefinite leave to remain
ILR is leave to remain without any time limit, and is a form of settled status. It can be granted at the later stages of various immigration applications, such as family migration visas. ILR used to be granted if an asylum claim was recognised, but this has now been replaced by 5-year refugee status (after which you can apply for ILR).

Home office
The government department for policies on immigration, passports, counter-terrorism, policing, drugs and crime. The Home Office is headed by the Home Secretary.

Refugee
The word refugee has several meanings in international contexts, and in popular usage. In legal terminology in the UK, a refugee is someone whose asylum claim has been recognised under the Refugee Convention and who has been granted status (leave to remain).

Reference- Right to Remain

The following pages represent just some of the many images and art work created by the young people during the workshop process.

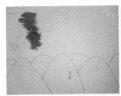

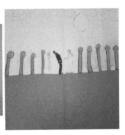

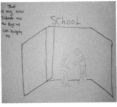

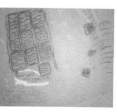

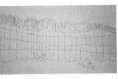